# The Norfin® Trolls

## The Best Costume Party Ever

by Mitzy Kafka

SCHOLASTIC INC.

New York   Toronto   London   Auckland   Sydney

**Designed by Charles M. Hervish**
**Photography by Mary and Joe Van Blerck**

ISBN 0-590-46958-4

12 11 10 9 8 7 6 5 4 3 2 1     2 3 4 5 6 7/9

Printed in the U.S.A.          37

First Scholastic printing, November 1992

Ingrid and Ivan looked out the window and softly sang,
"Rain, rain, go away. Please don't come back another day."

KNOCK KNOCK!
Hey, here's Hector. Everybody calls him Einstein because
of his crazy hair.

"What's up, gang?" asked Hector.
"Nothing's up," Ivan said, "and we're down."
"There's nothing to do," explained Ingrid.

"Nothing to do?" cried Hector. "I can solve that problem. Let's throw a costume party!"
"Einstein!" they exclaimed. "You're a genius!"

All the Norfin Trolls pitched in to help plan the greatest costume party ever. Some made invitations.

Some helped decorate.

Some baked cookies and cakes...

while others just clowned around!

Finally the day of the party arrived.  DINGDONG!
Hooray, the first guests are here!

Wow! Talk about making a splash.
Look at that fabulous mermaid outfit!

"Yar, me laddies!" cried a mystery guest.
"Shiver me timbers!"

Abracadabra!
Here's someone dressed as a magical wizard.

And look!  Up in the air.... It's a bird, it's a plane,
it's...it's...an astronorf!

DINGDONG!  DINGDONG!
More and more guests were arriving.
"I'm having a ball," said a happy Troll in a baseball costume.

"Darling, you look heavenly."
"Thank you," said Angel.
"Your costume looks pretty hot, too!"

It's no mystery who this guest is.
He's Sherluck, the famous detective!

It's a golfer and a leprechaun. What a stroke of good luck!

Hooray! The singer is here. Be-bop-a-lu-la!

Then Ingrid yelled, "Hey, everybody!  Let's Rock and Troll!"

The Trolls danced and sang. They even did all the old-fashioned dances, like the monkey, the mashed potato, and the jitterbug!

But everyone was wondering who would win first prize for
the best costume. Would it be the fire fighter? Or the nurse?

How about the cheerleader?  Or the police officer?

Maybe the cavewoman would win. But it could be the tourist...or the bride and groom.

There were too many great costumes to choose from!

Shh! Quiet, everyone. Hector wants to make an announcement. The Norfin Trolls gathered in hushed silence. Who would be the winner?

"My best friends," said Hector. "You all look so wonderful, we can't possibly choose just one winner. So we decided there's only one thing to do. . . .

"Jelly beans and balloons for everyone!"
A cheer rose from the crowd.

Then somebody cried, "Party on, Trolls!"

And do you know what?
That's exactly what they did!